W9-BHR-232

STORM

BY W. NIKOLA-LISA
ILLUSTRATED BY MICHAEL HAYS

Atheneum   1993   New York

Maxwell Macmillan Canada
Toronto

Maxwell Macmillan International
New York   Oxford   Singapore   Sydney

Text copyright © 1993 by W. Nikola-Lisa
Illustrations copyright © 1993 by Michael Hays
All rights reserved. No part of this book may be reproduced or
transmitted in any form or by any means, electronic or
mechanical, including photocopying, recording, or by any
information storage and retrieval system, without permission in
writing from the Publisher.

Atheneum
Macmillan Publishing Company
866 Third Avenue
New York, NY 10022

Maxwell Macmillan Canada, Inc.
1200 Eglinton Avenue East
Suite 200
Don Mills, Ontario M3C 3N1

Macmillan Publishing Company is part of the Maxwell Communication
Group of Companies.

The text of this book is set in 16 pt. Bodoni.
The illustrations are rendered in acrylic paints.

First edition
Printed in Singapore
10 9 8 7 6 5 4 3 2 1

Library of Congress Cataloging-in-Publication Data

Nikola-Lisa, W.
Storm / by W. Nikola-Lisa; illustrated by Michael Hays.—1st ed.
p.   cm.
Summary: A farmer and child watch as a thunderstorm sweeps into
the valley, surrounds them, and then rushes off again.
ISBN 0-689-31704-2
[1. Thunderstorms—Fiction.] I. Hays, Michael, 1956– ill. II. Title.
PZ7.N5885St   1993
[E]—dc20   92-22775

To B.C., the storm of my life
W. N-L.

For Heather
M. H.

Storm.
Blue sky darkened.
Green fields checkered.
Yellow sun streaked with clouds
and hiding.

FLASH!
Lightning in the hills.

RUMBLE!
Thunder right behind.

FLASH! RUMBLE!

FLASH! RUMBLE!

FLASH! BAM!

RUMBLE!

CRASH!

The wind is whipping through the trees.
The rain is bouncing off the ground.

The world is dark and wet outside.
Suddenly the storm is all around.

The storm is all around
and all you can hear
is the rat-tat-tat
rat-tat-tat
of raindrops
beating down.

The robin huddles in its nest, waiting.

The cows in the field stand still.

The farmer stares from his window
as water races past his
newly planted seed.

The world is dark outside.
The world is wet,
 and wild with the wind
 that shakes the house,

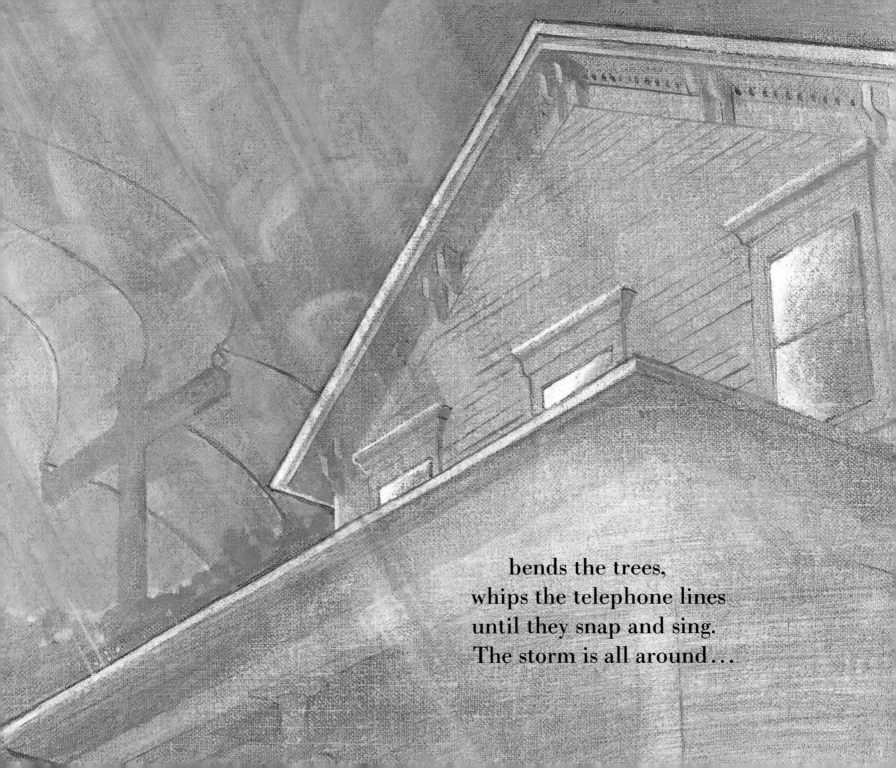

bends the trees,
whips the telephone lines
until they snap and sing.
The storm is all around...

the storm is all around.

Then a hole in the sky opens.

The robin in its nest looks upward.

The cows twitch their tails in the field.

On his porch the farmer chuckles to see
the hole grow bigger

and bigger

AND BIGGER!

Until it fills the sky again with blue,
and paints the fields with green,

and drenches the sun with yellow so bright

it almost hurts to see
    the storm,
now just a lace skirt draped
over the distant mountain rise

...and quiet.